It Came from the Morgue

D.L. Winchester

Winchester Horror Publishing

For the nurses & staff at the Pecos, Hamlin, and Fisher County Hospitals.

Jesse

JESSE PUSHED THE STRETCHER down the basement hallway, wondering if they'd ever replace the burned-out bulbs in the fluorescent lights. He understood *why* they put the morgue in the hospital basement, but it didn't mean he had to like it, especially with only a couple flickering bulbs to light the way. Why couldn't the funeral director just come pick up the bodies when they passed, instead of waiting until the morning?

Because he's a lazy motherfucker, just like you!

The morgue was the only room down here still in use, and the hallway had been converted to storage for old medical equipment. He wheeled the gurney past a pair of spare beds, and noticed one had a sheet and blanket on it.

Someone's been sneaking down here for naps.

Probably Danny, the night shift janitor. They never could find him when they needed him. Jesse would have to remember that. Maybe even tell Deidra, the charge nurse.

If she caught Danny, there'd be hell to pay, and as loud as she was, there'd be plenty of entertainment for everyone else. The fact that Danny was her little brother only meant the rebuke would be that much stronger.

In rural hospitals, you made your own fun.

Reaching the double doors that led to the morgue, he went around the gurney to prop them open before returning and pushing the body inside.

The steady hum of the refrigeration unit greeted him, and he kicked himself for leaving his sweatshirt upstairs. It wasn't the first time he'd forgotten how cold it was down here. He pushed the gurney around the corner to the body cooler. There were nine slots in the morgue wall for bodies, eight more than they usually needed.

Whoever designed this room had been optimistic.

Or pessimistic, depending on your perspective.

Jesse opened the center space and pulled out the sliding rack. Positioning the gurney so it was next to it, he grabbed the sheet-wrapped body and pulled it onto the metal tray.

This one was light, thank goodness. Not all of them were. One had even broken the rack, sending the body crashing to the floor as Jesse jumped out of the way.

Walking to the wall, he picked up the clipboard with the log on it and carried it back to the body. He found the toe, where the morgue tag was supposed to have been applied upstairs, but there wasn't one.

Fuck.

Deidra would chew someone's ass about that too, but at least it wouldn't be his. The day shift nurse was supposed to apply the tag, since the time of death was before shift change, but the nurse was new and probably didn't know.

Not that it would spare her from Deidra's wrath.

Undoing the sheet the body was wrapped in, Jesse began looking for the hospital ID bracelet on her arm. If *that* was missing, there'd probably be another body down here shortly.

He pulled the sheet out of the way, revealing denim-covered legs, then a faded yellow tank top. As Jesse uncovered the dead woman's chest, his hand brushed against something.

A nipple, he realized. They were poking up against the fabric, unrestrained by a bra.

They were really nice tits, he thought, finding the tag on her wrist and copying "Jane Doe" onto the clipboard. Out of curiosity, he pulled the rest of the sheet off, revealing a young, pretty face with blond hair splayed around it.

Probably a college student. MVA from the highway.

There wasn't a lot of blood, if that was the case. Or any visible injuries.

And damn, her tits looked nice.

He put his hand under her tank top, sliding it over her left breast. It was firm, kind of small, but the erect nipple felt good in his hand. It'd been years since he'd touched an actual human breast (it wasn't his fault no woman this side of Amarillo wanted to fuck him), but the familiar high quickly returned—elation, followed by relaxation.

This is wrong!

She's dead! I'm not!

Jesse lifted her shirt, exposing the woman's body. He'd have to be quick, but if anyone came looking, he'd hear the elevator bell and have plenty of time to cover her up.

Pulling off his gloves, he tossed them at the woman's feet, then dropped his pants to the floor. His cock was already hard, even with the slight chill in the morgue.

This is wrong!

I'm just jerking off, it's not like I'm actually fucking her!

God, it felt good. He stood over her, his hard cock in one hand, his other hand feeling her breast. Fucking heaven. Maybe it was better when they were dead. No stupid moaning about it hurting or wanting to change positions or pulling out.

Too bad most of the dead people were old, ugly bitches.

He felt the sensation build in his cock, and when the pressure became too much to hold in, he released, sending squirts of jizz across the dead woman's skin.

"Shit!" he muttered.

It did look kind of hot. Some even landed on her tits.

Down the hall, he heard the bell ring.

"Double shit!"

Pulling his pants up, he walked across the room to the sink and grabbed a wad of paper towels. He used them to clean the woman as best he could, then pulled her shirt down, threw the sheet back over her, and slid the tray into the cooler.

Goddamn, that was nice.

He washed his hands, then put on another pair of gloves. Getting some more paper towels, he grabbed the bottle of sanitizer spray and went to clean the gurney.

Thunk!

Had that come from inside the cooler?

No, that was impossible.

Thunk!

Or was it?

It could just be a rat; that had happened before. Jesse reached for the door handle. He could go report it, but Deidra would just laugh and send him back down here to deal with it. Might as well save himself a trip.

Thunk!

He pulled out the rack, and the woman sat up.

Jesse stumbled backwards, tripping over the gurney and sending it and him crashing to the floor. Thank goodness for the noise, he thought as he tried to untangle himself. Maybe whoever came down here would come investigate and see this resurrected bitch smiling down at him.

As Jesse watched, she used her finger to scrape a glob of his cum he'd missed off her chest and put it in her mouth.

"Delicious."

Her voice was slow, lower than he expected. It almost sounded haunted, but that word didn't describe it right either.

Demonic.

That was it. That was the word.

Fuck.

"I'm glad," Jesse stammered.

She swung her legs off the rack, and dropped to the floor. She pulled her tank top down, and Jesse could see her nipples were still erect, probably from the cold air of the cooler.

Or maybe…

"You taste good." She leaned over, letting Jesse see down the front of her shirt as she whispered in his ear. "I want more."

"Aren't you dead?" Jesse asked.

"Could a dead woman do this?" Placing a hand on either side of Jesse's head, she pressed her lips to his. Jesse tried to push her away, but she was too strong. It felt like his entire body was detaching from his skin and being pulled out through his mouth, but that wasn't right. He could still move his hands and feet, could still push against her, even if it didn't work. Everything fucking hurt as he tried to resist, tried to stop whatever was happening.

In a moment of intense pain, he felt himself separate from his body, then he was falling in darkness, through darkness, with no form.

Then he was gone.

★★★

"Delicious," the woman said, standing up. She looked down at Jesse for a moment, then her body started changing. Bones lengthened, skin expanded, her light hair turned dark. The woman's face morphed, her features changing in a swirl of motion until she looked like the man she was looking down on.

Danny

DANNY HEARD A CRASH from the morgue and sighed. Damn Jesse. It wouldn't be the first time he'd dropped someone on the floor trying to transfer them.

At least this one was dead.

He knew he should probably go help the guy, but fuck. If a thirty-five-year-old who had been a CNA for fifteen years couldn't figure out how to move someone from the gurney to the morgue rack, that sure as shit wasn't his problem. And as soon as he tried to help, his sister was liable to make it *his* problem from now on.

Fuck that.

He stretched out on the bed, intending to take a nap. So far, Deidra hadn't found him down here. And as long as he kept his radio at full volume and appeared when she called, she probably wouldn't be down here to check. Which was good. About the only place left she wouldn't think to look was the morgue, and Danny wasn't sure how comfortable one of those racks would be.

They couldn't be much worse than these old beds. He closed his eyes. Whoever designed hospital equipment left a lot to be desired, he decided as he drifted off.

Danny opened his eyes to find Jesse standing over him.

"Jesus! Fuck!" He sat up quickly, banging his head against Jesse's. "What the fuck do you think you're doing, man?

That's some messed up shit, trying to scare me."

"I'm not trying to scare you," he replied, rubbing his head where Danny'd hit it. Danny furrowed his brow. It looked like Jesse, but something was off. "Jesse brought me down here."

"Are you high? Stop messing around, dude." Danny wondered if the night shift had finally pushed Jesse off the deep end. "Who'd you drop in the morgue? I heard the crash."

"A vessel. The beginning of something greater than she could even imagine."

"What the fuck, man? Why are you talking like that?" Danny scooted back on the bed, ending up against the cinderblock wall. "It's really starting to freak me out. Can't you be normal?"

"This is the new normal," Jesse said with a smile. "Jesse set me free, brought me to life with his seed. Then I consumed him for nourishment. He was delicious.

Now, his body is more than it ever was before."

"You're crazy," Danny muttered.

"You have no idea," he purred.

"Enough of this fucking bullshit," Danny said. "I heard you crash the gurney."

"Jesse did that," he said, shrugging. "He is no longer with us."

"Yeah, well, where the fuck is he, because Deidra is going to whip his ass."

"I told you," Jesse said, leaning across the bed toward him, his eyes suddenly glowing red. "He was delicious."

"Jesus, fuck!" Danny kicked his leg out, sending Jesse's body into the hallway's far wall. Whatever was controlling it went along for the ride, and Danny hoped his little flying lesson would fuck it up enough to let him escape. Climbing off the bed, he took off running down the hall.

What was that thing? What the fuck did it mean, Jesse was delicious? Did it eat him?

A hand grabbed his foot, and he tumbled to the door a few yards short of the staircase. Danny tried to get up, but the Jesse-thing had shifted its weight to his knees, preventing it.

"Look, man," he stammered, trying to roll onto his back. "This was a funny joke, ha ha. But come on, you've taken this far enough, haven't you?"

"This isn't a joke."

Danny's heart raced in his chest. "Look, you already, what did you say, 'consumed' Jesse. He's a big boy. There's no way you're still hungry."

"I'm famished," the voice came in his ear again, as it climbed on his back.

"Come on," Danny said, wishing he hadn't knocked his radio to the floor when he got out of the bed. The hospital's security officer would be a big help right now.

The Jesse-thing chuckled. "That's what started this." Another whisper, close enough he could feel its breath on his neck and smell the beginnings of decomposition in it. "You're mine now."

Danny flung his elbow back and caught nothing but air, but the motion generated enough momentum to roll him over. A moment later, it was back on top of him, using its hands to pin his arms to the floor.

"Silly man."

"What the fuck are you?" Danny asked.

It leaned down, its lips almost touching Danny's. "I'm a soul sucker."

He didn't have time to scream before it consumed him.

Deidra

Deidra looked at the messy trauma bay in the emergency department and sighed. Jesse had been downstairs for ages, longer than it usually took him to deliver a body to the morgue. Maybe he'd decided to go back upstairs to the inpatient floor and leave the mess to her?

He fucking knew better, Deidra thought as she reached for the phone. For a motor vehicle accident, it wasn't *that* big a mess, but it was the principle of the thing.

Give an inch, and they'll take a mile.

Deidra's grandmother had been the first to tell her that, and it was as true then as it'd been that day, sitting on the back porch shelling peas. Danny had tried to sneak inside before the garden was weeded, and Grandma had sent him back to finish the job.

Speaking of Danny, she hadn't seen him either. He'd found a new hiding place, and she hadn't had a chance to look for it.

The emergency department only had two rooms, enough for her to handle on top of her charge nurse duties. If she needed help, she could always call upstairs for one of the CNAs or LPNs to come down.

Census was low again. Only one patient upstairs, leaving fifteen rooms empty. That worried her more than anything.

The next closest hospital was forty-five minutes away, forever in an emergency. Even with the straight, flat roads of the Texas Panhandle, the ambulances could only go so fast. Their hospital was a lifeline for their county and all eleven hundred souls that occupied it.

Where the fuck was Jesse?

She reached for the phone and pressed the button for the upstairs nurses' station. It rang twice before Linda answered.

"Yes, ma'am?"

"Is Jesse up there?"

"Nope. Haven't seen him since you called him down."

Deidra sighed. That meant he was still down in the basement doing God knows what. "Okay, I'll go track him down."

"He probably fell asleep on one of those old beds in the basement." Deidra shook her head. She'd been telling the administrator they needed to get rid of that old junk for years, but they never seemed to get around to it. "We beat Miami, by the way, 86–40. Tyler had three touchdowns and an interception."

Deidra rolled her eyes. Six-man football, as good a way to fill up her emergency room as any other in their sleepy town. Tyler, Linda's grandson, was a senior and one of the star players.

Luckily, the team was on the road tonight, which might have something to do with why things were so quiet.

"That's great," Deidra said. "I'm gonna go see if I can find Jesse."

"Good luck."

She got up and headed for the staircase. There were a few old beds down there, and they might be where her brother liked to hide too. Maybe she could kill two birds with one stone…

★★★

Deidra opened the door at the bottom of the stairs and saw Jesse on top of her brother, kissing him.

"What the fuck is going on?" she demanded.

He looked up at her, a grin crossing his face.

"I don't know what you're smiling for. This is what I need to finally get your ass fired!" Deidra snapped.

Getting to his feet, Jesse began to change. He closed his eyes, and when he opened them again, Danny's green eyes stared back at her. His hair started falling away, until all that was left was Danny's gray halo around a bald top. The nose and mouth twisted, then sprang back as Danny's. The torso filled out, arms and legs lengthened to match her brother's height.

Her brother lay on the floor behind the shapeshifter, but he also was the shapeshifter.

Deidra screamed.

The stairwell door clicked shut behind her, and she turned to open it. Strong hands grabbed her, and pulled her back into an embrace.

"So delicious." Her brother's voice, but not his words. It licked her neck and she whimpered. "Where were you going?"

"Look, just let me go, please," Deidra stammered.

"Why?"

She was nine again, her brother holding her down as he forced her to eat a bug or a worm. "This isn't funny!"

"Of course not." It pushed her against the wall, turning her around before closing the distance between them.

Deidra didn't hesitate. She rammed her knee into her brother's crotch, as hard as she could.

No reaction.

"You think you can hurt me?" His face closed in, stopping inches from her own.

"What you consider pain is pleasure for me. And that was a perfect appetizer…"

Mike

Mike sat in the security office in the hospital's admin wing, keeping half an eye on the computer screens on his desk. The hospital only had a couple dozen cameras, focused on the entrances and patient areas.

The job was boring, an easy way to pad his pension after thirty years with the Amarillo Police Department. Coming back to his hometown for retirement made the most sense for a divorced man whose two college-aged kids wanted little to do with him—unless they needed money. That way, he could help his aging parents in their twilight years, while still being close to his kids if they felt like reaching out.

Which was rare, but better than nothing.

The main enemy he faced was boredom. Aside from the occasional rounds, there wasn't a lot to do. Nothing happened out here in the sticks; the only reason the hospital had a security guard was their insurance policy required it.

He'd just turned off the radio as the high school football game ended and picked up his book when he heard the scream.

At least, he thought it was a scream.

A moment later, his phone rang.

"Security."

"Did you hear that?" Linda asked.

Mike couldn't help but smile. Linda was another advantage of living back home. In high school, she'd been a senior while he'd been a freshman, and she wouldn't even look at him. Now, with her widowed and him divorced, her car spent a lot of time parked in his garage.

She was still in great fucking shape, and as smart and funny as ever. Definitely worth waiting thirty years for.

"The scream?"

"Yeah."

"I did."

"It sounded like Deidra. She just went down to the morgue to look for Jesse."

Mike sighed. Shit like that was supposed to be his job, but Deidra had an independent streak. "Want me to go check on her?"

"If you don't mind."

He smiled. "When I'm done, you want me to come check on you?"

A giggle. "If you want."

"I want," he said, hoping he'd be able to steal a kiss, maybe cop a feel.

"My grandkids are coming over tomorrow night, but if you want to come home with me in the morning…" she offered.

"Of course."

"Perfect. I'll see you soon."

Mike hung up and got to his feet. He didn't mind keeping his relationship with Linda a secret. Earl had only been dead three years, and Mike had been back home for two. Just enough time to ease into things, and let the old ladies down at the Baptist church begin to suggest that Linda should "get back out there, maybe with that nice retired policeman."

But it wouldn't be easy for her, he knew, especially with the grandkids. They'd just come to terms with Earl's death, now how did you explain to them that Mimi had someone new in her life?

He shook his head as he hit the button for the elevator. Maybe they were making it harder than it had to be, but it was what made Linda comfortable.

The elevator door opened, and he stepped inside.

Down into the basement. He hated it. It reminded him of an old insane asylum, cinderblock hallways and claustrophobia. The upstairs wasn't much better, but at least there were windows. There'd been talk of building a new hospital, but it would be a few years, Mike figured.

The door opened, and lying in front of him was Danny.

"Fuck!" Call it cop instinct, a gut feeling, whatever you want, but Mike's hand automatically went to his gun.

Except it wasn't a gun.

It was a taser, because he wasn't a cop, he was a night watchman.

"You can carry if you want," his boss, the retired sheriff, had told him back when he started. "Most of us don't, though. There ain't no need."

Now he felt a need, and his Colt was locked in the glove box of his truck.

The door started to close, and he put out a hand to stop it. He took a deep breath, then stepped into the hall.

Looking to the right, he saw Jesse lying on the ground. Slowly, he turned to the left and saw Deidra leaning against the wall, her hands on her knees.

"Shit." She looked up at him and smiled. "Getting smaller is such a pain."

Something was wrong. She should be on the floor, trying to help Danny, not smiling at him.

"What the hell's going on?" he asked, stepping over Danny to be on the same side of the hall as Deidra. If he had to use the taser, he wanted to be close.

"Danny and Jesse are dead," she said.

"Is that why you screamed?" Mike asked.

"I didn't scream. The woman screamed."

"What woman?" Mike asked, looking around. He saw Deidra lying on the floor behind Deidra.

Two Deidras? What was going on?

"The woman whose body I stole," Deidra said.

"Are you sure you're okay?" Mike gripped the taser tighter. It was pointed at the floor for now, but the more he heard, the more he wanted to use it.

"Never better." She stepped toward him, and he raised the taser.

"Stop!" Mike snapped. "What the fuck is going on? Why are there two of you?"

She laughed. "I've been feasting, and you're next on the menu." Deidra, if it really was Deidra, looked at the taser in his hands and shook its head. "You think that thing's going to stop me?"

Mike fired.

But Deidra was gone. The taser's barbs clacked off the wall.

The next thing he knew, something grabbed him by the hair and threw him violently to the ground.

"Funny thing, the more souls I consume, the faster and stronger I get," the thing in Deidra's body said, kneeling next to Mike.

He swung a fist at her, and missed.

"You've got spirit." It bent over him, leaning in close. "Too bad it won't do anything for you."

The last thought that went through Mike's mind as Deidra's lips closed in was that her breath stank.

Linda

Linda tapped on the door of room eight next to the nurses' station, then entered. "Everything okay in here?"

A woman in a deputy's uniform was sleeping in a chair next to the patient's bed. She opened her eyes. "Oh. Sorry. I guess I dozed off."

Linda waved a hand, moving around the bed to the monitors. "You worked all day and came in to stay with your grandpa tonight. I think a little sleep is okay."

The woman smiled. "If you say so, Ms. Linda."

Abbey had been in her son's class in high school, a sweet girl back then, one she'd thought Jason might have a thing for. But as soon as she turned eighteen, she'd left home to join the Marines.

At first, Linda had thought she just wanted to get out and see the world, but two years after Abbey left, her older sister, Carissa, committed suicide, revealing in her note that their stepfather had been sexually abusing both of them.

The man lying in the bed sleeping had been the one to find Carissa and the note. No one had seen the stepfather since that night, twenty-eight years ago now.

Looking down at Tom Zimmer, Linda knew they never would find him.

Zimmer was in the hospital recovering from a bout with the flu. At ninety-six, he was still as sharp as ever, spending his time working the ranch with his son and grandsons. He was a tough guy, but as he got older, bugs like this were a little too much for him to recover from at home.

"Everything looks good," Linda told Abbey. "How do you like being home?"

"It's different," she said, smiling. Even though she was no longer a marine, twenty-some years of habits died hard. Her brown hair was still pulled back into a tight bun, and her sheriff's department cap sat on the table next to her chair. "When a town like this is your world, everything is a big deal. But when you leave and come back, you learn a lot of the things people worry about aren't that serious, but some of the things you take for granted don't exist in other places, and coming back to them is as much of an adjustment as losing them."

"You'll be alright," Linda said with a smile. "If you need me, I'll be down at the nurses station."

"Thanks, Ms. Linda."

Linda sat down and checked her phone again. Her daughter's family was on the way back from Miami, not the city in Florida, but the small town across the Panhandle. She wanted to be sure they hadn't had a problem on the two-lane roads across the plains.

She looked up at the elevator indicator. It still showed B for basement. Mike should hurry, she thought. Though when it came to dealing with Deidra and Jesse, who knew what he was untangling down there? Those two could go at each other like a pair of tomcats fighting over a puss in heat.

Earl. That'd been one of his phrases. She still missed him, even though he'd been gone three years. As much as she loved Mike, he didn't fill the hole as much as he was pulling her out of it. There were still some days it was all she could do not to spray some of Earl's cologne on her pajamas, curl up under the blankets, and spend the whole day grieving.

They were married thirty-two years, thirty-two wonderful years. Five kids, twelve grandkids, and a couple more on the way. Life had treated them well.

The elevator indicator changed, going from B to 1, then 2.

Linda checked her reflection in a small mirror on the desk, then put on a smile as the elevator doors opened and Mike walked out.

"Did you find Jesse?" she asked.

"Damn idiot," Mike muttered, walking toward the desk. As he got closer, Linda noticed his taser wasn't in the holster like it usually was.

"I think you dropped something." She pointed.

He looked down, then shrugged. "It's not as important as you."

Her heart leapt. God, when he said things like that, it just made her feel light as a feather. "Come here, Sugar, and give me a kiss," she said, keeping one eye on the door to Room 8 in case Abbey came out.

When he leaned in for the kiss, Linda almost gagged. He didn't smell right, like a rotten animal lying in the Texas sun. She opened her mouth to protest, but Mike's lips pressed against hers, and it was too late.

Tom

TOM OPENED HIS EYES when the nurse came in.

"Hello," he said.

His sinuses felt like someone had stuffed them with sludge. He looked at the chair next to the bed and saw Abbey's purse, but no Abbey.

She must be in the bathroom. He liked that she came to visit him after her shifts at the Sheriff's Department. She was a good girl, a kind girl, who deserved nothing but happiness.

A memory popped into his head, of a man who had caused Abbey and her sister plenty of misery, disappearing under cow shit and quicklime on a remote corner of his ranch.

That had been a good night.

He didn't know if Abbey knew who had made that asshole disappear, but she'd never seemed to blame Tom for what happened the way she did her mom.

Some folks in the Panhandle may be backwards as hell, but he'd tried to believe his daughters, granddaughters, great-granddaughters, and now great-great-granddaughters could do anything a man could do. Abbey had been a damn fine Marine, and now she was a damn good deputy.

He just wished she'd be more open about herself. Tom knew she was a lesbian, had seen Abbey having dinner with a woman down in Amarillo, holding hands and smiling like the happiest woman in the world. Hell, it reminded Tom of the way his wife, Joanne, used to look at him.

But she'd never come out to him or anyone else in the family. He wasn't sure who she was hiding it from, and hoped it wasn't him, but also knew it wasn't something he could force her to reveal.

The nurse was at his bedside now, but she wasn't checking his vitals on the monitor like she usually did. Instead, she was staring down at him.

"Something wrong?" he asked, the congestion making his voice low and weak.

Then he saw her eyes.

They weren't the kind eyes of the woman who had cared for him over the past week.

It was a monster.

Eyes tell you everything about a person. He'd learned that lesson in Korea, working as a medic. The eyes told you everything you needed to know: if they'd given up, if they were willing to go peacefully, or if they were going to keep fighting no matter how you tried to help them.

Tom only remembered seeing eyes like this once before, when he came across an emaciated coyote trailing his herd, watching the calves frolic and play, waiting for its chance.

These eyes were hungry.

He tried to call out, but his voice betrayed him. The nurse—Linda, that was her name—leaned over the bed.

Her head snapped back with the force of his fist hitting her nose.

She hadn't expected that!

From the bathroom came the sound of a flush, and Tom knew Abbey would be back soon. Maybe she could save him from whatever was going on here.

Linda grabbed his head and held it in place. She'd heard Abbey too, and whatever she was going to do, it was happening now.

She leaned in.

Tom heard the bathroom door open.

Then her lips were against his.

Abbey

ABBEY CAME OUT OF the bathroom to find the nurse kissing her grandfather.

"What the fuck?" she demanded.

Ms. Linda lifted her head, and one look at her grandfather told Abbey he was dead.

Motherfucker!

What had that bitch done to him?

Then the nurse started changing. Her body and limbs lengthened, the already slender frame becoming skinnier. Hair fell out of her head, the little that remained fading from brown to blonde to gray to white. Her face contorted into a grimace of pain, and when it stopped, Abbey was staring at her grandfather.

"What the fuck?" she asked again.

The thing that looked like her grandfather started around the bed, and Abbey didn't hesitate. She rushed into the bathroom, slamming the door. A moment later, far too soon to be possible, the creature in her grandfather's body slammed into the door.

Abbey twisted the lock, then moved across the room. She drew her pistol, pulling back the slide to make sure a round was chambered.

What the fuck was this thing?

Dalton would know.

Fuck.

She couldn't believe she wished *Dalton* was here.

He'd been the weird guy in her last military police unit before she got out. He wasn't really social, but the kid knew everything there was to know about monsters.

Since no one else wanted to partner with him and hear him ramble all night, he usually ended up with Abbey, who did her best to tune him out. But now, she was racking her memory, trying to remember if he'd mentioned something about a shapeshifter with super speed.

Something slammed into the door, putting a large crack next to the door knob.

Add super strength.

What happened to the nurse?

Fuck.

Fuck fuck fuckidy fuck fuck.

Another hit, the crack got bigger.

Abbey reached for the radio hand mic on her shoulder. She'd heard dispatch send Jim Branscomb, the deputy on duty, out toward the county line to run down some escaped cows as she was walking into the hospital. But maybe they could call in someone off duty.

Another hit.

She could see it now, her grandfather's eye staring at her through the crack. Without thinking, she dropped the radio, raised the gun, and fired.

It stumbled backward, out of view.

Why had she locked herself in here instead of going for the hall? That had been dumb, but she hadn't really been thinking when it happened.

An eye appeared in the crack again, but it wasn't her grandfather's.

It was the nurse's.

Soul sucker! Dalton's voice rang in her mind.

It had to be. He'd blathered on about them for a full shift one night. They checked all the boxes: the more souls they consumed, the faster and stronger they got, when they consumed (not ate, Dalton had been fucking clear on that) a soul, they took on the physical appearance of its owner, and it gained a life for every soul it consumed.

Its eye was still peeking in, and Abbey fired again, the sound echoing in the confined space.

With a shriek, the soul sucker moved out of sight. Then it hit the door again, and again, widening the crack but not presenting a target.

A hand reached through toward the handle, at the end of a hairy man's arm, and Abbey fired through the door where the body should be.

The hand disappeared. When it came through again, the hairy arm was gone, replaced by purple nail polish on neatly manicured nails.

Abbey saw it turn the handle, and the door swung open.

How many souls had the thing consumed already? She'd killed three, leaving eleven rounds in her gun…

It didn't matter. As soon as she saw the figure in the doorway, she fired once, twice.

The creature hit the wall opposite the door, changing quickly into a janitor, then the aide she'd seen earlier. It came toward her, moving slower than when it came around the bed.

Abbey fired again. Now the aide was gone, replaced by a young woman.

From the wreck. Abbey had worked the scene just before her shift ended, had helped load the girl into the ambulance.

"What's wrong?" Abbey asked. She knew the girl was gone, but part of her still wanted to save her.

"I need your soul!" the woman yelled, starting toward Abbey. But Abbey pulled the trigger, and the creature collapsed to the floor.

Abbey approached it, unsure if it was really gone. Dalton would know, but shit, she had no clue where he'd ended up.

Necrophilia creates them, his voice reminded her, though she wasn't sure why that was important. Had the aide done something stupid after the young woman passed? Was that why she'd had to deal with this…thing?

From the floor where she'd dropped it, the radio crackled. "Abbey, it's Denise at Dispatch, are you still at the hospital?"

She grabbed the handset. "Yeah, Denise, I'm here."

"I've got a report of shots fired, do you need backup?"

Abbey took a deep breath. What she needed was a good shrink and a fuck ton of alcohol. But backup would be a start. "Roger. Scene is secure, but backup would be nice."

"I got the cows," Jim's voice came in. "I'm on my way."

"You may want to call the sheriff," Abbey advised, stepping out into her grandfather's room and sinking into her chair. As she looked at what remained of her grandfather, a tear came to her eye. There'd been so much she wanted to tell him, so much she'd been robbed of the chance to. "I think it's going to be a long night."

Acknowledgements

Thank you to:
Milt Theodossiou for reviewing an early draft and assuring me this concept worked (also for all the awesome reviews!).
Chloe York for her editing expertise.
Ruth Anna Evans for the amazing cover.
Cyan LeBlanc for the insistence on going in a certain direction.
Wednesday for doing her best to add typos to the manuscript.
Atlas for staying out of the way and

watching YouTube.

Anna for all the love.

And you, dear reader, for reading this work!

About the author

D.L. WINCHESTER LIVES IN the foothills of southern Appalachia. A former mortician, his work searches the darkness to find tales worth telling. He is the author of over three hundred obituaries, numerous short stories, the novellas The Screaming House *and* Devil's Fork, *the novelettes* Dead Money *and* The Colony *and the collections* Shadows of Appalachia *and* A Terrible Place and Other Flashes of Horror.

D.L. also serves as the President and Associate Editor of Undertaker Books, an independent horror publisher. In his spare time, he can be found searching for inspiration in the world around him and helping his wife try to keep their children from becoming the next generation of horror villains.

Also by D.L. Winchester

Shadows of Appalachia
A Terrible Place
The Screaming House
Devil's Fork
Dead Money
The Colony
Mother Clucker
Night of the Chupacabra
It Came From the Morgue